FAE DEALS & OTHER TALES

FAE DEALS & OTHER TALES

A fantasy short story collection

GWEN TOLIOS

Libra Chai

Printed by Libra Chai

Contents

As Needed

Your daily workout has been a disappointment – four years of lifting and no progress. Hoping to end the day with some cheer, you hit up the local pub and, in a bizarre, drunken way to prove that you've made some progress, you challenge a tough-looking guy to an arm wrestling contest.

You break his arm and destroy the table.

You immediately apologize, though the man's friends' threats against you, the man's screams of pain, and the bar owner shouting at you to leave probably make it hard to hear.

The best course of action is to leave, so you do.

The entire walk home, you trace your hands, your wrists, your arms. You know they're the same size (you've been measuring your biceps) as they've always been. Glances in the shop windows as you go by confirm it.

Waiting for a long light, your still buzzed mind decides to conduct an experiment. You punch the brick wall next to you and immediately regret it. You feel that pain in your bones, even as you never felt the grip of the man while you sat across him at the bar table.

You cross the street, sucking on your scraped knuckles.

At your place, you realize that in your hurry to leave the

bar, you've lost your keys. Desperate to get home, you try to open the door anyway. You push the handle *through* the wooden door. The splinters don't bother you, your hand feels fine, and with a creak the door slides open around your hand.

You blink, sigh, and walk into the building. After a poor attempt to fix it with duct tape and gorilla glue, you resign yourself to telling the landlord in the morning and hope the other units in the building have their doors locked.

You pause at your unit's door and switch hands. You're just as desperate to get through this one, but maybe it's your right hand that is too much? But nope, your left does the same, and now you have to worry about paying for two damaged doors.

At this point, your beer haze has disappeared. Shock sobriety. You stare at the weight set you've been using for four years. It'd worked at first. You found it easier to lift things, carry groceries, and only needed to hit a nail once, even as your muscles stayed the same and the weights always felt as heavy. You plateaued ages ago, but the habit had been incorporated into your life and it was only recently you decided to stop in favor of running.

You look at your hands. Look at the weights. It had been a suspicious craigslist buy, complete with alley pickup. And it was a very unfinished set. One pair of dumbbells. One kettle ball. One bar with weights.

You pick up a dumbbell. It's the same weight as always, but for the first time, you pay attention to the faded words stamped onto the metal.

Mar Chumhacht Riachtanach. N lbs

You think it weighs ten pounds. Easy to pick up, but you'll feel the reps. When you place it on your bathroom scale -

another thing that hasn't changed as you presumably gained muscle - the scale says the weight is zero.

It's midnight, but you have no desire to sleep. You try to lift everything you can. You start with the fridge - no dice. But you can an hour later when you need it out of the way to pick up a fork that slid under.

You look toward the weights again. You don't know the brand, but type it into google. To your surprise, you get a translation.

As Needed Power.

Apparently, that man in the bar really did need to be taken down a peg.

Love Will Grow

Susie found the bag on her pillow the night after their third date. Small, made of dark blue silk, someone had tied it closed with a pink velvet ribbon. The attached title card read "Johnathon Maynard".

Susie immediately felt creeped out. Why would John leave a gift on her pillow? How did he even get into her house? Shit, did he take something?

She bolted upright. Leaving the bag on her pillow, she checked all the doors and windows. All were locked and nothing was out of place. Her laptop and iPhone sat undistributed on her desk. She still had eight teaspoons.

Assured of her safety and belongings, she took a closer look at the bag. The title card wasn't in John's chicken scratch handwriting. Instead, the letters were round, if tiny. She picked up the silk, marveling at the smoothness of it on her palm, but couldn't feel the weight of something inside. Susie flipped the card to read "love will grow" on the back before opening the bag. Inside resided a single, round, seed. An indentation on one edge and its rusty red color reminded her of a heart.

She planted it in an empty Jiffy jar, put it on the kitchen window sill, and watered it every day.

On the morning of her and John's two-month anniversary, Susie noticed the first bit of green sticking up above the soil. She stared at it in wonder while the coffee maker gurgled, turning the peanut butter jar cum plant pot around in her hands. Growing things had never been something she was interested in, but staring at this little sprout she felt pride and wonder at her ability to encourage the seed to sprout.

On their date that night, Susie decided John had long-term potential.

The plant grew, from a bit of green to a seeding two inches tall. When the first leaf unfurled, aiming toward the sun, Susie learned John could tell when she was upset and knew exactly how to make her feel better. This was officially a serious relationship.

Susie posted in forums about the plant, hoping for help identifying it, with no luck. Its description was strange, its lifecycle stranger. Since discovering the seed, she had planted several other plants that had already bloomed. But this John Flower, as she had taken to calling it, took six months to form a bud. Instead of green like she expected, the bud was burnt orange and covered in white fuzz.

She snapped a picture for her forum. Perhaps that could help someone identify it. But, just like her description of the seed, nothing came of it.

It was an odd little plant, but it was hers. She decided to introduce John to her parents.

The bud didn't bloom for months, just sat on the stem

collecting sun. Susie watered the plant and added fertilizer, but the bud didn't open and she wondered if she was growing food instead of a flower. No fruit or vegetable appeared, even if the bud swelled to the size of a fuzzy grape. Maybe that was it; the plant was done growing and would die soon.

It didn't.

A year after Susie met John, he proposed. She came home that night to find the John Flower had bloomed, the grape-sized bud expanding into a flower with an eighteen-inch diameter. Shaped like a sunflower, its pink petals turned a deep red near the center. The flower faced, of all directions, away from the window.

Amazed at the flower, Susie didn't notice the card against the Jiff jar at first. Written in the same rounded hand the first card had been, it simply read "Your love has bloomed."

Dear Deer

The knock on your backdoor is unexpected, more so is the...being... who answers. You cannot call them human, standing six feet tall with an extra ten inches of elk antlers growing from their head. Their hair is short enough that you can see the antler's bone root, and it's possible hair might not be the right word either. Fur?

Yet there's something familiar about the figure. The large, warm brown eyes. The nut brown of their skin. Their odd, blocky teeth. You stared at a kid years ago with teeth like that, they took your fascination for interest, and you had a ceremony there by the swings to witnesses of birds, a booger-eating kid, and a girl more interested in making her action figures fly.

"I intend to marry you and love you forever," the kid had promised, tying a long string of knotted grass around your wrists.

"Sure," you said back then, caught in the make-believe, but now, staring at this elk person you can feel that grass on your bare skin, hear the squeak of the swing's chain, remember the breeze that seemed to circle the two of you when you received a kiss on the cheek.

"Roosevelt," you say, the name coming back to you.

"Wendy?" the being asks, eyes alight with hope. "I've been looking for you for a year!"

"Well, you found me." You can't help how your eyes go up to the antlers, but you do your best to stop your gaze from going down to check for hooves. "Did, uh, oh shoot. Am I a child faerie bride?"

Roosevelt blushed and ducked their head, antler points scraping the door jamb. "Yes. I'm really sorry! For us, intent matters most in magic, and back then, in my childish ways, I meant those words truly. We've been married nearly fifteen years."

You swallow. You've heard the stories of kidnapped brides, the women who disappear at the hands of strange folk. "Have you come to take me away to faerieland?"

"What? Oh, no. That spell was a mistake, we were both so young. But it was binding, so I've come to ask for a divorce so I can get married to someone else."

"Oh good." You sag in relief. "I was planning on proposing to my girlfriend tomorrow. It'd be best if we're both officially, magically single."

Trumpet Wars

There were always rivalries in band class. The clarinet section hated the flutes, the saxes the trumpets. Tubas were just the cool people that got along with everyone, the rest of the low brass feeding off their coolness just enough to not be ignored while still being shuffled aside. And then it was all the winds versus percussion.

But that was normal school stuff. While the rivalries had been heated and fun during middle school and high school, by the time Ken hit university it was just an inside joke that only showed up in prank Christmas gifts and happy hours at the bar. Okay, and maybe the occasional joke on the blackboard, but that was the professor's doing.

Most of the time, they were just concerned with the music. Learning it, playing it, perfecting it, writing it. Ken and the rest of the music majors lived quarter notes and Italian speed phrases. He never had any problem with other trumpets, not even Janet who bumped him down to second trumpet. She, and the other three trumpets ahead of him, were a challenge.

His senior year of college, Ken felt animosity toward a fellow player for the first time. The Dungoo Symphony Orchestra, a top-of-the-line group that traveled the country, announced open additions. Ken would have traveled across three state lines to audition, but fortunately, his in-person evaluation would be on campus.

Ken was surprised at how many people were there warming up when he arrived. He thought the process would be more selective and that he wouldn't be going up against more than fifteen other trumpeters. Sure, this location was only one of seven in the country the DSO designated for in-person auditions but really? 50 others? He ran a finger over the schedule. 15-minute slots. Not long to show off his technical skills.

He arrived early, too early perhaps to warm up. Instead, Ken pulled out his trumpet, propped his sheet music up inside the case, and went through fingerings as he imagined the sounds. A vibrato on this whole note, double tonguing that run, circular breathing during that middle passage. Twenty minutes before his time slot, Ken figured he should start blowing wind through his trumpet.

As he fitted his mouthpiece on, he was suddenly aware of a harsh glare on the back of his neck. He turned around to see a Hispanic man, maybe late 20s, looking at him through narrowed eyes. Something about Ken riled him up, and now that he was looking at him, Ken thought the same thing in return. The man's darker skin, his uncombed hair, the color of his shirt, and, oh man that trumpet! Hadn't the other guy heard of polish?

Ken tried to shake off the sudden violent dislike toward someone he'd never met and blew air through his instrument to warm up the metal before running scales. Wanting to show the other guy he might as well pack up and go home, Ken made sure to use his best tone and went slightly faster than normal. His lips felt great, his trumpet was behaving as if it wasn't still warming up at all. Ken turned, looking out of the side of his eye at the other guy in a challenge.

When Ken paused for breath, the Hispanic man took over playing with the complementary minor scale. No, the blues complementary scale with its skipped notes and accidentals.

Ken did two octaves.

The other man did the same but in reverse.

On the same brainwave, they each took a deep breath and played C, trying to not be the first one to run out of breath. Even with circular breathing, Ken was running out of air, but he held out for half a second longer.

He sent a cocky smile to his newfound rival.

The other man looked murderous. Carefully, he put down his trumpet and stood up, looking as if he was going to sock Ken. Once standing, the other's face smoothed as his desire to start a fight faded. He looked as if he didn't know why he wanted to start a fight to begin with.

That grated Ken.

"What, not man enough to do anything?"

The man flopped a hand at him. "I've got better things to do." And with that, he sat.

As soon as he touched his trumpet, he pulled his hand back as if burned. He looked up at Ken.

"What?" Ken snarled at him.

Still looking at him, the other trumpeter took his hand on and off his instrument. The behavior was so odd, Ken's dislike of the other faded to confusion. What was he doing?

Before he could think of an answer, his name was called. Goodness, he was so caught up in competing he hadn't run any of his trouble sections. Too late now.

The other man was called too. The professor indicated they were to each stand outside a different door. Ken spent the time fingering until he was called into the room. Deep breath, he told himself. Think of it as an S&E competition, you rocked those.

The room was a small practice room, with not much space for more than a stand and a panel of three judges. Ken said hello and gave a little bow.

"Let's start with scales. Play C minor."

Halfway through the scale, he realized he could hear sounds from the other audition room. He knew exactly who was playing.

In hindsight, he didn't remember playing for the three DSO representatives. His entire focus was on the competition's sound and surpassing it. He didn't care if he didn't land a job with the orchestra, as long as he was better than the other trumpet player. He had never felt so passionate about playing his best. He had also never played as well. Tone, breathing, color, technique; he had never gotten this close to perfect playing. Grudgingly, he attributed his performance to the other man. But only after the audition while giving his trumpet a quick polish.

As Ken closed his case, he noticed the other man also getting to leave. He didn't know what had sparked the animosity he felt towards the other player, but maybe getting to know him would help. Ken jogged over to offer his hand. "Hi, I'm Ken Price."

"Conor Caraballo."

They shook.

"Look, man," Ken began. "I felt extra competitive today. Not sure why, but I just wanted to let you know it wasn't your fault."

Conor nodded. "No big deal. Hey, try something for me?"

Ken shrugged yes.

"Look at me without touching your trumpet, and then while you are."

It was a crazy suggestion, but Ken was willing to humor Conor. He felt bad about thinking so little of him before. Ken sat on a chair and pulled his case onto his lap. With a snap, he released the catches. He hovered his hands over the trumpet and then looked at Conor, paying attention to his opinion of the guy.

Kinda friendly and maybe a little bipolar, but a pretty darn good trumpet player.

Ken placed his hands on the trumpet.

Conor was a no-good show-off who shouldn't be because he had no skills to show off in the first place. He smelled, cheated, and manipulated others to gain ranks in groups, he -

Ken took his hands off the trumpet. "That was...weird."

"You're telling me."

"Our trumpets make us hate each other?"

"Did you hear yourself? That's crazy."

"Yeah, but..." Ken trailed off, looking at his instrument before slowly closing the case. "You have any other ideas?"

"No. Just that I'm gonna ignore it and hope I never see you in a situation like this again. And now, to make up for all that anger I felt toward you, I feel like I should buy you a beer."

"I know just the place."

Water Childe

Mom pulls the keys from the ignition and we stare out the window at the cabin. I hope coming here to clear it out will wash away my last memories of Grandma.

"I can't die without my fur coat. I can't die like this. I know he hid it, I know it. Can you find it?"

"I'll look Grandma. Promise."

As the Alzheimer's set in five years preceding her death, as her ability to distinguish me from my mom faded, Grandma asked for the coat every day. Now, whenever I think about her, I see her frantic eyes and feel her panicked fingers digging into my wrist.

The family cabin in British Columbia is supposed to bring to the surface happy days from my childhood coming to visit Grandma and Grandpa. It is supposed to rinse away the feelings of pity I now feel for Grandma's lost mind and my guilt at my unwillingness to see her.

I just see a cabin on the coast. Nothing happy comes to mind.

"Thanks, Lea, for coming. It would have been nice if your dad came too."

I hum in agreement. I couldn't blame Dad, cleaning out

the cabin to prepare it for market is sure to be a messy, emotional affair for Mom. So would scattering ashes in the ocean. Still, I couldn't let Mom come alone.

The inside of the cabin is dusty. My last time here, my freshman year of high school, it had been clean from constant summer use. But then Grandpa died and family reunions ceased. The last people to visit had been Dad and his biking buddies, years ago.

I don't want to think about the dust. I want to think about Grandma. I want to picture her smiling face.

Mom and I set our bags down in the master suite before starting the long process of organizing the items in the cabin. We make piles for the small things – keep, toss, sell – and label the big ones with masking tape. The realtor Mom is working with arranged for an estate sale on Memorial Day. There should be lots of people seeking items for other cabins in the area, though Grandma and Grandpa's has always been isolated.

I look out the kitchen window at the rocky shore. Grandma used to stand here and stare out the window, her gaze distant. I mimic what I recall her doing every morning as she made coffee - reach over the sink to grab the window knob and crank it clockwise to open the window.

"Good morning, brothers and sisters," I whisper.

When Grandma did it, the seals' barking would fill the kitchen as if they were saying good morning back. Now, it's early afternoon and the rock islands off the shore are empty.

What strikes me about the sudden memory the most is that it's not what I expected. This is something I have seen Grandma do hundreds of times and child-me remembers smiling at it. I had thought Grandma smiled too, but imaging her in this same spot a decade ago I can't recall her smiling. She was wistful.

Mom walks in from the front room, books in hand and a fond smile on her face. "Look what I found! My mom used to read these to you when you were younger, do you remember?"

She hands them to me, the dust gritty on my palm. Some of them I only recall because they have sat on the shelf for years – picture books about beach trips and mermaids – but I know the red, pleather-covered book with the silver embellishments.

It has the boring title of Folklore Tropes. Grandma embellished the stories every time she read them to me; I had thought the book was magic with ever-changing tales until I learned the truth. It was a non-fiction text of bland examples of mythology tropes: animal brides, trickster spirits, fairy godmothers, great floods.

"Can I keep this one?" I flip through the pages, sneezing at the dust released into the air.

"Just the one?"

"Just the one."

"Okay. I think I'll keep a few myself. For my future grand-children."

I roll my eyes but smile.

That night, when I'm flipping through the folklore book on the couch and Mom is reading a mystery on her Kindle, I ask something I'm not sure why I never asked before.

"At the end, Grandma always talked about a fur coat. But I don't remember her having one. Do you?"

"Oh, yes. When I was little she had a few. Dad gave her

them. But she always said they weren't hers and wouldn't wear them. Why she... she went on and on about one at the end... I just don't think she knew what she was talking about. Why would Dad hide a fur coat from her?"

I nod and return to my book.

I wake up before Mom the next morning, make myself tea, and walk down the short front yard to the start of the beach. In reality, it is a bunch of boulders scattered along the coast where waves splash constantly. A full five feet of small nooks and crannies crammed with tide pools between the grass and ocean I used to play in. Grandma never played with me.

I wonder why she wished to have her ashes placed in the sea.

Mom mentioned, once, when I asked as a child, why Grandma never stepped onto the rocks. She was scared of the power of the waves. But as I stand here, feet close together and staring at the seals on the rocky islands a few hundred meters out, I can see Grandma in my mind. Short, coarse hair. Round belly and face, though her chin and nose jutted out. Her arms tight against her side. Her large brown eyes looking past me and Grandpa playing to the seals and looking sad.

I shake my head as I walk back to the cabin, mug half full and tea cold. Why did this cabin only bring me unhappy images of Grandma? These were worse than my memories of her in the nursing home. My memories of the cabin were happy. Had Grandma never been happy here?

No, she must have been. She wanted her ashes here after all.

As we finish the living room and go through the boxes in the closets, I pay particular attention to the photos we find of Grandma. She doesn't smile in any of them.

"Was Grandma never happy?" I ask.

Mom answers with a laugh and a kiss to the top of my head. "Lea, your grandmother always had trouble expressing emotions, but I know she was happy."

I make a noncommittal noise of agreement.

In the afternoon we start on the loft, the "kids' room". Mom takes the shelves and dressers, fawning over childhood knick-knacks and clothes. I catch her tossing a ratty stuffed seal, fur rubbed off around its neck, into the trash pile.

"No, Mom. I want to keep Ariel."

"She's filthy and old, Lea."

"I don't care." Looking at that stuffed animal I can remember my fourth birthday. Grandma smiling at me as she says, "Seals are my favorite, so I expect you to take good care of her." That day seals became my favorite animal too, and Grandma gave me many versions of them over the years. Ariel though was the first and you always keep first things.

It strikes me - this might be the only memory I have of Grandma smiling. I hold it close.

"When we get home, she's going straight into the washing machine," Mom says.

I sigh and turn back to the closet. It's full of more kid clothes; brightly colored winter coats and scarves, tiny boots, and rain slickers. There are also old blankets and a shelf at the back full of 250-piece puzzles and board games with boxes falling apart at the seams. I smile, remembering rainy days playing with them, and add them to the sell pile on one of the twin beds. Some future kid will love them.

When I go back to start opening the boxes on the high shelves above the clothing racks, I see the wooden panels behind them have warped and bent, making a gap through which I can see a bit of blue.

I know if I look out of the room's window I can see the ocean, but today it is a dirty gray. I am seeing something else. Intrigued, I stick my pinky into the gap and am surprised to feel cloth.

Together, my mom and I move the shelf, pull out the nails in the panels, and expose the back of the closet. There, hanging on a hook and wrapped in blue cotton, is a fur coat.

We know without a doubt who it belongs to.

I watch my mom reverently stroke the front of it. "What do you know, she did have a hidden fur coat."

"She said Grandpa hid it. Why would he hide something so beautiful?"

It's both right and wrong to call the coat beautiful. For something my grandmother obsessed over for years, it doesn't seem like much. It wouldn't be on display in a store; it lacks the long, shiny strands that bring to mind a fatty diet. Grandma's coat has short, coarse fur a dapple gray that reminds me of the seals that bathe on the rocks. It isn't a coat one would stroke for a luxurious sensation or wear for warmth.

However, it is one of a kind. Despite Grandpa hiding it away and Mom never seeing Grandma wear this, it is worn, thin. I have never seen an article of clothing that feels so magical. It makes my fingers tingle. Hiding it away feels like a good thing to do. Something so nice and important needs to be kept safe. At the same time, something in my chest sings at the idea of it being out in the air, of being found.

Why Grandpa hid it behind the wall in the closet, or why he had never given it to my grandmother despite her desire for it, I don't know.

"Try it on," Mom says, passing the coat over. "It looks too small for me."

Reverently, I take it from her. I slide first one arm in, and then another. I smell the sea, feel as if I have been lying on a flat stone for an hour while reading, and suddenly I want to swim.

Mom places a hand on each of my shoulders and strokes them down my arms over the fur. It feels as if she is touching my bare skin.

"You look beautiful in it. You should keep it."

"You don't think we should release it in the water with Grandma's ashes? She wanted it so badly." Even as I say it, I know I want nothing more than to pull the fur coat tighter to me and burrow into the collar. It should be mine. I want it to be mine, and the coat itself seems to mold to my skin, claiming me. I feel bad instantly.

"She won't miss it. And such a beautiful thing should be used." Mom caresses the fur again.

"Okay."

#####

We go down to the shore the next morning, the car already packed and ready to go, to say goodbye to Grandma in the early morning light.

I wrap the coat around me. It's been impossible for me to let it out of my sight.

The water laps up against the large boulders we climb over

while attempting to avoid tide pools. The seals are barking on the rocky islands a few hundred meters from the shore, louder than I have ever heard them at dawn.

I imagine they are calling to my grandmother in the newspaper boat Mom has carefully tipped the ashes into. Grandma had refused to touch the water, never going farther than where the sparse grass meets the first rocks.

Once as a child, I asked her why she never went closer. She said it was forbidden. It didn't stop her from etching the same view of the horizon with charcoal every trip to the cabin and hanging them in every room of their home.

"Bye, Grandma," I say to the paper boat in my mom's hands as I crouch on a slippery rock.

"Bye, Mom," my mother whispers and gently places the paper boat on the water. The tide is going out. Grandma's ashes will swim through the sea in a way she never had.

The seals are barking, and something about it is musical. Their harsh calls have always been a sound of my childhood summers, but now I hear a melody. A tune that rolls in its up and downs of both rhythm and pitch. It's a sad song of the sea, but at the same time, it's welcoming.

I can hear words.

Come home, come home, Eaura. Your memory will be eternal as the sea. Come home, come home, Eaura. Sister, you are with your family. Be at peace.

They tug at something beneath my breastbone. A call, a pull. *Come home, come home.*

The seals aren't just singing to the ashes in the boat. They are singing to every part of my grandmother and the coat on my shoulders is tingling.

I slip on the rock and Mom catches me. "Careful," she says. "I don't want the sea to take you, too."

But it's too late. *Come home, come home.*

I slip forward, no, it's a step, no a waddle, because my feet don't exist anymore. I'm shrinking as I'm diving, the fur coat merging from clothing to skin and then I'm in the water swimming, swimming, following the boat of ashes that has moved so far away in such a short period of time.

"LEA!" My mom screams.

Home, home! The seals sing as the ocean pulls.

Mythic Souls

I knew from a young age the only job that would satisfy me was something violent. The army would work, lots of guns and killing for glory, but the action wasn't constant outside of war. And while I loved the idea of being on the front lines, I knew no war was forever and eventually I would need more violence.

It was as necessary as air for me to keep my sanity. I had to fight, and if possible, use explosives to do it.

I joined the army anyway. Earned a reputation as a pyro-maniac, trigger-happy, son-of-a-bitch, but still made it to the elite forces. But the violence wasn't enough, the missions my unit went on were too passive and too few. As the years went on, I needed more and more violence to calm my soul and when I couldn't get it from missions I turned on my unit. I blew up our safe house with 10 pounds of C4 on a mission in Turkey. I had put a mug under each of their beds before pressing the trigger to collect blood. Only two didn't break, and neither were full – should have used bowls instead for a wider collection hole – but I drank the blood they collected nonetheless.

Needless to say, I was declared rouge and became a wanted criminal.

Working freelance was much more my style. A kill almost every week, once I had built up a clientele. There was no need for a vacation; killing, and killing violently, was my joy. I gained a reputation for dealing out gruesome deaths by fire.

But then, on a hit in Tokyo, I saw you. And I knew you were different, like me. You didn't have your own soul either.

I followed you. I never saw you angry, though your job as a peacekeeper for the UN had to be stressful, and you had a sucker's heart. You might have suspected that the poor kid trying to sell you gum was going to pick your pockets, but you bought from him anyway. You also had a soft spot for young girls, enough that I would have called you a lesbian pedophile if I hadn't watched you take men to bed.

In addition, you were paranoid about your health. You only drank filtered water and had a portable filter for tap water. Your bathroom mirror had a supply of vitamins behind it and you only bought organic.

I broke into your hotel room one night; you were in Beirut and hoping to help with peace talks between Israel and Palestine – again. I took one look at you, with your pale skin, bleach blonde hair, and sapphire eyes, and knew you as soon as you walked into the suite and saw me sitting in the middle of your bed.

"You're a unicorn."

And you said, "You're a dragon."

I hadn't been aware of you watching me as I watched you, so something had to have given me immediately away. Maybe you could smell the blood on me from a recent kill, or maybe you had sensed the danger you were walking into and picked the most dangerous mythical creature known to be reborn into a human. Or maybe it was a power of unicorns, to know what type of mythical soul they were looking at.

I had only been identified as a dragon twice before. Once by myself when I realized where my violent tendencies came from. Another, when I killed a man I hadn't known for a phoenix. He came back minutes later to spit out my identity as a curse. In both cases, the realization had been met with a display of what it might mean to be a dragon. As a human I couldn't fly, but my soul belonged to a dangerous predator who knew its way around fire, quick strikes, and long blades.

But you, when you said it, I did not feel the need to show you what being a dragon meant. You, or maybe your other soul, looked past that to the darkness at my core. All mythical creatures are of a darker nature than humans or animals, even one as peace-loving as a unicorn. Their souls were born in a darker time when they weren't allowed to live in peace. Mine is full of violence and yours, yours is full of self-loathing because you know traps but you walk into them anyway.

I don't know what that connection felt like to you, that one night we met, but it reminded me of the time I set the kitchen table on fire and my parents sent me to a boarding school for difficult children. I'd felt human until the moment I stared at the flames, something I never thought I would ever feel again until I stared at you.

The next morning, you were gone before I woke and left a note saying that while you knew I could find you, you would appreciate it if I didn't. *You* wanted to find *me.* I looked forward to it.

Still, I was terribly upset at losing you. I blew up a bank, I'm sure you saw it in the news. And I've found myself since you left needing violence even more to placate the dragon inside. You looked at it, at me, saw the darkness deep inside, and stayed even if it was just for a night.

Next time, I'll make you stay longer.

Deeper Underground

Even before his fifteenth summer, Daniel knew he wasn't a city boy. But now, smack dab in New York City he was face-to-face with the one place he didn't want to be.

The city reeked. Homeless people, methane, trash. It also was deafening. Horns, shouting, radios.

His first night, he thought he was going to go crazy from sensory overload and the depression that followed. If he couldn't get revenge for Lacy, then he might as well try to find a coven or nest that would put him out of his misery. He had planned on assisted suicide to begin with, but had hoped to make a kill or two first.

But it was impossible to follow the scent.

Daniel didn't have anything specific to go on; the only spilled blood in the forest belonged to Lacy and the pack. There had been the scent of gunpowder and a tang in the air that spoke of silver. He hadn't seen the bullets. Silver was expensive. The hunters had dug it out of the bodies of his family and in the process skinned them. Daniel returned to find the three of them with muscles showing, flies feasting. Without their fur, it was only the scent of their blood that identified what body was who.

The only helpful scent had been oil from a car, and he traced that through the woods until he came to the city that never slept. It was an awful place, where the stars were barely visible and he couldn't make out the surface of the moon. He still felt the lunar pull, but he missed being bathed in moonlight. The street lights were too bright to allow for that.

There was no direction for him to follow and everything was so strange. Daniel wondered aimlessly, stumbling through alleys and tunnels, digging through the trash.

But last night...

Daniel's nose was always sharper as the full moon approached, even in human form. He had scented that oil, a large amount, and followed it. It wasn't the first time, many cars in the city seemed to use the same and like usual the trail led to an auto shop. But the shop he found last night smelled of more than oil, grease, and metal. There was another scent, fainter, that came from a corner in the back. It was covered in parts when Daniel found it, but under the smell of the shop was the faint whiff of soap, and fainter still, of blood and fur. Both of which he intimately knew.

Lacy. Steve. Natalie.

And others, the smells so faint they had blended together with age and he couldn't make out individuals. But Daniel knew his pack wasn't the first to have their wolf skins laid across that table.

Wolves were smart animals, using tactics to fight as a team and bring in a kill. But they were also wild animals, who didn't have sophisticated emotions or morals. As a result, since his fifteenth summer, Daniel only felt the basics. One emotion at a time, and they were all-consuming.

It wasn't the full moon, but he could still call up a partial shift.

Daniel's knees switched direction, his thighs bulking up while his calves slimmed. His hips and chest expanded, the muscles growing as coarse, copper fur sprouted over his skin. The shirt he wore was tight, itchy. It ripped with his expanding chest and he tore off the rest of it with his muzzle.

He was still humanoid, standing on two legs. His face had a wolf's snout, but his eyes and ears were more human than wolf. He wasn't the large wolf creature that hunted in the woods, but he still had teeth and claws and lost himself to violence.

Daniel read in the paper the next morning about what he'd done. The garage was ripped apart, the family living above it killed. He noted that the article used words like 'creature' and 'monster', making statements about paw prints and claws. Everyone knew about his kind, but it was an unspoken rule to not mention them. Saying the name of any supernatural was supposed to bring bad luck and death on its heels.

He expected the nests in the area, maybe some of the covens as well, had known he arrived in the city, but this public attention concerned them. It explained the silver-wearing girl under a parasol at the end of the alley. The man following him since lunch who flashed a pointy smile when Daniel looked over his shoulder.

New York City's others lived alongside humans because of their ability to hide. Daniel had destroyed that. Now they were either going to kill him or toss him out of the city.

The full moon was coming. He would be at his strongest,

as would be the covens, but the nests would be weak. Even so, one werewolf couldn't stand for long.

The warning displays would be enough to send anyone else off, but Daniel couldn't leave. He may not remember killing that family, but rage over his pack's death hadn't disappeared.

Right now, the city was panicked. While those fanged smiles were for him, he wasn't the only one seeing them, not with the humans hyperaware after that article. The panic was good, he hoped it would flush out more butchers, but it wouldn't do to have attention on him. He needed to go to ground, someplace close to the garage to watch who came and went, and come the full moon he would hunt.

Then, and only then, would he allow himself to be caught. To die.

Fairytale

"I swear, it's like a fairytale." Courtney swung me around, not minding the other people in the lunch line. She bumped into Scott Noble, who turned and glared at her. It cowed her, but not much. Her body stopped moving, but her mouth didn't.

"I had no idea what to do. Here I am, stuck at the gas station, with a full tank and a flat tire. And because it's after midnight, the guy behind the counter wouldn't leave it and help! The best he said he'd do was keep an eye on my car if I pushed it away from the pump for the night. And if I came back at the shift change at seven, he'd help me put on the spare. But I didn't trust that. I mean, sure, I'm sure he'd watch it and all that, but he can't see everything. So I asked for a 24-hour tow company, to see if someone could at least take it to a service shop because I figured, hey, there it would safe and in no rush to be fixed. I'd just get a ride home, and to school the next morning with you."

I nodded in the right places, making noises while I told the lunch lady I wanted pizza. Mondays the school got it from Gino's Bakery and Gino made the best pizza for miles around.

"You listening, Diane?"

"Yes, you couldn't figure out what to do about the flat tire." My hand hovered over the mini-fridge. Water or orange juice? The school had gotten rid of pop a year ago.

"Yes! And so there I was, flipping through the yellow pages when this college guy walks in, and I can tell cuz he's wearing the school's sweatshirt. And on a whim, he just looks at me and says, 'that you with a flat tire' and oh boy, Diane, his voice was like chocolate. And his eyes were a piercing gray, never thought gray eyes pretty before I saw his. But they were like mercury, liquid silver, and I swear I just stared open-mouthed at him. Didn't realize I was gaping until the counter guy answered for him. I couldn't believe I embarrassed myself like that!"

I grabbed a cookie. I needed a treat after listening to her latest boy drama.

"Anyway, the college guy, William by the way, asks if I have a spare, and I say yeah, but I don't know how to change a tire. So he said he'd do it for me. Took off his jean jacket, mum, those arms, and figured out what all the stuff in the emergency kit was. Boom, not ten minutes later the spare is on the car! I gotta hit the service station after school today, but hey, I drove home with Mom none the wiser! I asked what I could get William for his trouble. I was thinking a beer, no way the gas station guy was gonna give my fake a double check, but you know what he asked for instead?"

"A million dollars?" I said, sitting down at the end of our usual table. Courtney pouted as she sat across from me.

"No, a kiss. And a token to remember me by."

I raised my eyebrow. "Did this kiss lead anywhere?"

"That's what makes this such a fairytale! He only kissed

my hand! And took that fake flower pin I had, saying every time he looked at its fake beauty he'd be reminded of how my face outshone it threefold. Who says such things, threefold? Anyway, his last name is Prince. William Prince. Now don't tell me he doesn't sound dreamy."

"Actually, he does. Did you get his number?"

"Yup," Courtney pulled out her cell phone. "We've been texting all morning. He wants to take me to a movie to-morrow night."

"Go for it! And ask if he has another gentlemanly friend."

#####

"So?" I asked Courtney in the hallway on the way to lunch. She was practically glowing.

"It was amazing. I mean, we didn't pay attention to the movie of course, but he insisted on paying for dinner, which was at this super fancy place. I should have dressed better. And he paid for the tickets and snacks. But you know what, he saved me again!"

"Really?"

"Yeah, walking back to his car this huge dog attacked us. It grabbed a hold of my skirt and pulled. It slipped off my hips and oh Diane, my underwear was exposed to the entire parking lot! It was awful! But William picked up this steel pipe on the ground and poked the dog in the side as if it was a sword. The dog took off, leaving me on the cold ground with my skirt halfway down my thighs and William standing over me. But I swear, just like Prince Charming would do, he helped me up, completely ignoring my underwear, and just asked if I was alright. God, he's a dream. He saved me from a modern-day dragon."

"Wouldn't that be a giant lizard or something?"

She hit my shoulder. "I'm being symbolic here! He's saved me twice now! If that's not a prince in shining armor, I don't know what it is. Like I said Monday, I'm living in a fairytale."

It was probably because I just came from English that I remembered Ms. Flagg's tidbit about fairytales.

"Did you know fairytales were originally cautionary stories? You know, warnings not to go into the woods or talk to strange people."

Courtney snorted. "Ariel and Aurora and all those princesses ended up living a happy life. If anything, fairytales are about what you gain by being a good person. Which I totally am."

I wanted to say something about how while Disney movies might have happy endings, the stories had not been as pleasant. The Little Mermaid committed suicide. Aurora was raped while asleep and woke up during childbirth, only to die during the procedure. Good people didn't always win, even if the Huntsman saved Little Red Riding Hood and Hansel and Gretel killed the witch.

But really, what a stupid thing to be thinking about. Detroit might be a dangerous city jungle, but Courtney was streetwise enough to know when a stranger was dangerous or not. Female intuition and experience.

Sunday night, I heard soft taps at my window. Courtney throwing candy at it; we found out years ago using rocks was a bad idea.

I opened it to see her standing at the base of the tree that grew near my window. She was pale, bundled up tight in her coat and scarf, hand clutching the navy fabric close to her neck. It wasn't *that* cold.

"Court?" I whispered. I might be up, but my parents had gone to bed recently.

She looked up at me with pleading eyes and my heart melted. "One moment, can't climb down in shorts."

I traded my sleep boxers for sweatpants, then crawled through the window. From there, I slowly made my way down the tree. My jump landing startled Courtney from her grass gazing. I could make out tears in her eyes, the heavy mascara on her eyes.

The blood on the scarf.

"Courtney?" I said, grasping her shoulders. "You're bleeding. Do you need a doctor?"

She shook her head. "It's small, just a band-aid would do."

Nodding, I uncovered the spare key to the backdoor and let us in.

"What happened?" I demanded, tip-toeing to the bathroom, my hand on her wrist. Her skin was icy cold. I flipped the switch and we both winced at the sudden light. Once my eyes readjusted, I commanded her to sit on the toilet and went searching under the sink for band-aids.

When she didn't say anything, I knew something was really up.

"Courtney?"

"You know how you said fairytales are warnings?"

I had to think back to the beginning of the week. "Yeah." I drew out the word, not sure where this was going, and pulled out the med bag.

"Well, I... I should have figured the one I was living in was too good to be true." She pulled down her scarf.

Her neck was smeared with red and now in the bathroom light, I could see just *how much* blood her scarf had absorbed. More than enough for Courtney to be woozy and unsteady on her feet, but she had been fine entering the house.

"Shit," I said, forgoing the band-aids to reach for a washcloth. Courtney's hand on my wrist stopped me.

"It's a lot of blood, but that's not the problem."

"Not the problem!"

"William...he, he bit me. See, he's *is* a prince, and it's given him certain powers." Courtney pulled back her lips, and I watched her incisors grow.

(Dis)Connect

We met in college, both so unsure of ourselves, but we figured it out together. Okay, my meddling roommate helped too. And your insistent mother. But, eventually, we discovered who we were as adults and during the process discovered our compatibility.

Our post-college plans already involved a move to the East Coast to start our adult lives, so it made sense to propose during our graduation ceremony. I wouldn't have made it through school without you, just like I knew I wouldn't make it through life without you. We were too busy kissing to throw our caps.

But within a year we learned that who we thought we were, who we grew into during our four years of tertiary education, was only part of our true selves.

There was a reason we had been drawn together. Like attracts like, and we were the only two demigods on campus.

You have muse blood, so you've been trying to find and connect with this new aspect of yourself. You joined a writer's group, auditioned for commercials and shows, take ballet. When you showed me a clay mug you made at a studio last week, pride in your eyes despite the uneven rim, I saw your joy. You claim everything you try feels right.

I'm happy for you, I truly am, but this new inner person you are discovering differs from the one I knew in school. You come home late, you miss dates, and you developed alternative names. A stage name, a pen name, a dance name. Sometimes, I feel as if with each new name you become a different person. You aren't Judith Park anymore. You're Delilah London, Cleo Koula, Samantha Trabotii.

You are finding yourself again, but this time without me.

I wouldn't say you are leaving me behind, for I am doing the same. I rise every morning to do sun salutations, and I volunteer at a local therapeutic riding center to be near horses. With all your discovery adventures I can't fund my own, but the center lets me ride for free so I don't pay for lessons. I only ride occasionally, but I'm a natural and all the horses at the center love me. If I weren't saving for our wedding, I would save for a mount.

Rising with the sun, greeting the dawn, is my way to connect with Apollo, but you don't seem to notice. You expect me to *oo* and *ah* over your artistic creations, but you don't apply that attention to detail to me. You've refused every invitation to a morning yoga session, sunrise viewing, sunset picnic, and visit the barn.

You are involved with your creativity so much you quit your job at the bank.

You no longer answer when I call you Judith.

You are no longer the woman I fell in love with.

But I cannot be angry for your change of character, because you are still you, just a different version.

Plus, I changed too.

As I watch you sleep tonight, I am also saying goodbye. Just as you've been exploring your connection to the gods, so have I. The sun chariot is real, and I've been offered a chance to drive it for a year with my father.

Goodbye Judith. Or Delilah. Or Cleo. Or Samantha. Whoever you are when you wake this morning. I used to love you. I still do, but it has changed as we did so I'm taking that ring back.

Heaven's Threshold

"You can't wait outside the Gates." He told the soul that appeared a minute ago.

"But Gabriel, I promised my wife I would wait for her so we can enter Heaven together."

He wasn't Gabriel, his name was Fernando Munguia, but he didn't bother correcting the soul. Lore said the angel Gabriel guarded the Gates of Heaven, so they all assumed he was the fabled angel. Even though he didn't have wings. Or give off an aura.

He did however have a flaming sword. He supposed that accounted for the misidentification most of the time.

"You can wait on this side. The clouds shift over there, you'll fall through. Don't wanna fall to Hell waiting for her do you?"

"No."

"Then walk through the Gates."

The man did and promptly forgot about his wife.

Once you crossed the Gates, your mind went blank. You forgot about your life on Earth, and thus any ties to people there evaporated. A soul could walk side by side with their first lover and not know it.

It hadn't bothered him when he'd been appointed as Gate-keeper. Someone had simply pointed him to the booth just inside the Gates, led him inside, sat him down, and put a piece of paper on his lap.

"This is your new job," the someone had said, "and it's described in this paper."

It simply read: *Make everyone walk through the Gates of Heaven.*

He questioned none of it until he met Kanno.

Kanno had faded in like souls do, in the appearance they held as they died. He was a small Asian boy, hair in an uneven cut, clothes sopping wet until his soul morphed into its ideal image. The wet clothes changed into a set of robot-printed pajamas and he turned a year younger. Usually, at this point, a soul realized they were dead. Not Kanno.

"Yoko! Yokooo!" the boy spun around frantically, tears in his eyes.

Fernando sighed, thinking what a hassle. This soul wouldn't go through the Gates on his own so he had to go out and get him.

It was the first time he stepped outside of Heaven. The first time he remembered his name.

Fernando Munguia.

The thought was so startling he dropped the sword, clouds hissing as the flaming weapon hit them. Worried they would evaporate and leave him nothing to stand on, he hurriedly picked it up.

He looked toward the boy. He had stopped crying, eyes wide and staring.

"I'm Fernando." He felt compelled to say, to share.

"K-kanno." The kid stammered back, eyes on the sword.

Fernando wanted to do something else, but the only thing he could think of was that piece of paper: *Make everyone walk through the Gates of Heaven.*

He gently pushed the kid toward the Gates. Kanno resisted, asking where Yoko was, but Fernando kept shuffling him forward. "Yoko is just beyond the gates."

Kanno ran towards them but slowed to a sedated walk as soon as he crossed the golden threshold. He went on silently.

Fernando suddenly dreaded walking through the Gates, but the sword was burning his hand and the only safe place for it was in the booth.

#####

He hadn't forgotten the encounter with Kanno. Well, he did forget once he crossed the Threshold of Heaven, but the next time he went beyond the Gate it came back to him. Kanno. His name.

Now, he remembered all the time, in the booth or not. And it seemed each time he crossed the threshold he gained new knowledge – how mountains formed, how long a mother carried a fetus, how to boil rice.

Knowledge souls arrived with but had whipped from their minds.

But no matter how often Fernando crossed the threshold, he couldn't remember Earth.

#####

A woman garbed in a hospital gown faded in lying flat on

a cloud but after a few rattling breaths stood. Her appearance changed, short white hair becoming long and red, done up in two buns at the base of her neck. She wore faded green jeans under a short, strapless sea-green dress.

She saw the Gates, they were impossible to miss, but she dismissed them to look around the clouds. "Walter?" She called out.

Fernando stepped out of the booth and into her view. She turned to stare at him through the golden bars in the shape of ivy.

"I'm looking for my husband Walter. We promised we would meet here."

Fernando nodded.

"Have you seen him?"

"It's been a while since he arrived. The clouds on that side shift too much, so he built this booth to wait in. He's sleeping, but I'm sure he would like it if you woke him."

The woman smiled and skipped through the Gate, but she walked past the booth without a second look.

Fernando stared at that sheet of paper tacked onto the wall of the booth. Why was it so important that people enter Heaven? Why did they have to forget? Was it the same way in Hell? Was there some type of limbo?

Couples regularly made promises to meet at the Gate they never kept, but something about the most recent woman made him pause. The memory of her triggered a strange sense of familiarity.

A green dress, long and ruffled, and love for the woman in it.

Had he made a similar promise?

#####

He didn't know how long he stood outside the Gate, watching the shifting clouds while straining to remember something else about the woman in the green dress. Souls appeared and Fernando sent them along, but he found himself drifting closer and closer to the cloud edge. The fog was too thick to see through, but it didn't prevent him from trying to catch a glimpse of something. The blue of Earth's water, the fires of Hell. Something. He was tired of white.

#####

A couple dressed in camouflage appeared on the clouds. They were wrapped around each other, covered in wounds. They were shortly followed by another soldier, leg blasted off.

The couple ignored him. They unwound from each other, eyes wide as they watched their appearances change. Wounds disappearing, camo fading away to dress uniforms. They started kissing.

"This Heaven?"

Fernando turned his head to see the single soldier staring up at the Gates. Most people saw themselves at their prime in their 20s, but he had transitioned to a young teenager wearing khakis and a pale pink polo.

"Yeah," Fernando said, "Just through the Gates."

Popping his collar, the teen strolled through the opening.

Just after he was through them, the man in the couple yelled. "Wolf! Wait up!"

The young boy didn't turn around.

The soldier turned to look at Fernando. "That common?"

Fernando nodded.

"The draw of the Pearly City too much for most people?" He smiled and looked down at his partner.

"It's not really a pearly city, more cloudy," Fernando said. "And it's not a draw. You forget things in Heaven."

"Forget?" The female soldier echoed.

Fernando nodded. "Everything including your name. It's supposed to bring peace."

"I'm not going in, Joe," she said. "If you're right behind me, and I don't know you..."

Joe pulled her tighter just thinking about it. "Me too, Gloria." He looked at the cloud edge.

"What happens if we jump?" he asked Fernando.

"No idea. But I must insist, go through the Gates. It's not worth the risk."

"I think it is."

Gloria nodded against his chest and then they were running off the rim of clouds. Fernando rushed to the edge and watched them fall into the fog below, spread out as Xs and clasping hands.

#####

Fernando stared at the piece of paper. It glowed, that one sentence the only thing he had to do and the one thing he had failed. *Make everyone walk through the Gates of Heaven.*

Gloria and Joe threw away a chance of happiness to remember one another.

He thought of the woman in the long green dress.

He ripped down the paper. Or tried to, it refused to rip, but he was able to pull it from the wall. The magical paper fluttered as it fell to the floor, not even wrinkled. Fernando stared at it, breath heavy, then looked up at the wall it'd been tacked to. There, carved into the booth, were the words *Heaven's not enough.*

Fernando thought about his predecessor for the first time. Had he jumped?

He ran his fingers over the words. The only thing that could have possibly carved them was Gabriel's flaming sword, but Fernando could never handle the weapon with the finesse required to carve such smooth words small enough to fit behind a sheet of paper.

The angel Gabriel himself?

Fernando walked through the Gates, stopping at the edge of the clouds, praying for some sign of what he should do.

A name floated up the fog, Juliana. *Her* name.

He dived off the clouds.

She used to come to the school's swim meets.

Paper Burning

"Words have power," Carradoc said, voice carrying to all sitting around the fire. "With words, you can do anything. You can control a man's heart, tame a beast, or change your form. A skill with words will get you what you want, but the noblest use of the silver tongue is to praise the gods and goddesses. That is why druids use their skills to worship, and why the best speakers are druids."

He proceeded to tell the tale of the children of Lir. In testament to his silver tongue, the fire's shadows helped tell the tale. The silhouettes of the four children writhed as they were turned into swans and when Carradoc talked of their beautiful voices the fire didn't crackle but sang sweeter than any bird. I looked back and forth between the fire and the shadow actors, trying to see the shapes in the flames, but the fire looked the same as it always did.

If anyone could help me, he could.

As the rest of the village slipped away to their homes, I crept closer. While several families offered their homes for his short time in the village, Carradoc refused them all. He wanted to sleep under the stars with a bed of earth, he said.

I'd done that often enough and would have taken the roof.

I waited for him to stir the embers of the dying fire before I spoke. "Um, hello Druid Carradoc."

"Hello, dear." He continued to watch the embers, and I took the extra seconds to make sure my bruises were covered and tame my hair.

I shuffled closer to the fire. "I was hoping you could help me with something."

Carradoc looked up. I expected the same look in his eyes as the rest of the villagers when they see my dirty body and ratty clothes, but his face held no emotion and I felt as if he saw the me from five years ago, healthy and well taken care of.

"What do you need help with?"

"The story you told, about Lir's children from Aeb... I have a similar problem."

"You and your twin are going to be cursed into swans by your aunt."

"No, Druid." How to explain to a stranger I was the village orphan, taken in by my uncle who did all he could to see that I died without committing murder? That I only ate when other families were kind enough to give me scraps, and only slept warm when nestled next to wooled sheep?

I twisted my hands and Carradoc sighed.

"Come closer, child."

I moved into the weak firelight. The druid's eyes roved over my stringy hair and my dress straining against seams repaired many times. I ducked my head, embarrassed.

"How can I help?"

"Can you make my problems disappear?" I had so many.

Lack of food, lack of bed. Maybe Carradoc could make my uncle love me. Or stop his heart. Maybe he could turn me into a swan, and I could fly to a better place.

Carradoc dug into his small pack and took out a scroll. He unrolled it, keeping it in place with small stones, then coaxed the fire to come alive again. He stuck the end of a stick in the flames and when it charred handed it to me.

"Write your problems. The ones bothering you this very moment."

I grasped the charred stick and began to write; the charcoal marks an uneven color. Carradoc looked over my shoulder as I wrote. Hunger. Old clothes. No bed. Being dirty. Bruises. Cold.

Nodding, the druid took the parchment and held it over the small fire. "Fire, element of rebirth and destruction, gift of the life bringing Sun, destroy this past and bring a new future." He dropped it in the fire.

I watched as the flames licked the edges of my list, then it all lit up in a burst of heat. It was quicker than any other burning I had seen. I watched paper ash fly into the air and mix with the wood ash from Carradoc's early storytelling.

"Now what?" I asked.

Carradoc smiled. "Look at your dress."

It was no longer dirty, and all my patched holes had disappeared. Forgetting Carradoc was so close, I pulled up my dress to look at my thighs. No bruises. The ones under my sleeves had disappeared too. There was a new, steadily growing warmth in my belly that spread through my limbs.

Carradoc smiled my wonder. "When you walk home, you'll discover a bed and a meal waiting for you."

I took his hand in gratitude. "Thank you, thank you so much, Druid Carradoc."

"Of course, child. In a year or two, you can think of joining my order."

I nodded. After all, I'd just become a loyal follower of Bridgit.

Family Hauntings

Your daughter is old enough to scare the monsters under her bed.

"You can't scare me tonight!" you hear her say from the hallway. It's cute, but you miss being the one to shout under the bed. "My bedroom is my safe space and I say no scaring."

"I'm sorry," something says back.

More than the shock of hearing *something* answer is the fact that you recognize the voice. It's your father's.

Amelia has never met your dad. She wouldn't have recognized it. But you know that smoker's scratch. You don't know the tone.

After all, your dad never apologized to others.

You lean against the wall just beyond the doorway. Peek into the room. It's dark, but in the light from nearby streetlights you can see Amelia is in a squat, Minnie Mouse covered knees near her nose. She sits facing the bottom of her twin bed, one small hand lifting the bed skirt. You can't see anything under the bed, the skirt's in your way, but their conversation continues.

"Why are you hiding under my bed? I don't want you there."

"I can't be anywhere else."

"Not even closets?"

"No. Beds only."

Amelia frowns.

"Why are on only talking to me tonight?"

"This is my first night here."

"Oh. Well. You sound nice. You can stay."

"Thank you."

Amelia scrambles into bed, you can't do the same. You want to go in there. Drag out whatever is under your daughter's bed. But she has such a hard time falling asleep, and she's nearly there. Instead, you slide down the wall and sit there for the rest of the night.

Your back and butt regret it the next morning, but while Amelia skips off to brush her teeth and wash her face, you take your chance. You step into her room, drop on your belly, and lift the bed skirt.

It looks like it has every time you've seen it.

"Dad?" You ask. "Fredrick Herndon?"

"Hi, Lily."

You tear up. You can't help it. It's been years since your dad has said your name.

"What are you doing here?" you whisper.

"I saw a chance to see you again. So I took it."

You don't push for details. You're not sure you'd get them.

"Are you staying for long?"

"As long as you want."

"Then always, Dad."

You stick a hand into the darkness. A familiar hand grasps it.

Dream To Wake

It's a drunken question from a drunken night, living off the stress of finals your sophomore year. The prelim work is done and next year you'll be deep into the heart of your majors. No more sporadic art class, no more film analysis.

"Who here would be most likely to survive the zombie apocalypse?" Katherine asks, passing around the bottle.

There's a few hemming and hawing, but eventually, they settle on you.

"It's because I go deer hunting with my dad, isn't it?" you ask and they all nod.

It's a good answer, but you know that surviving zombies is not related to how good you are at sniping.

"Who here would be most likely to survive the aftermath of the apocalypse?" Brad asks after his sip of the bottle.

Again, the group points to you.

"It's because when I do go deer hunting, I'm roughing it for a week, right?"

"You hunt, clean, and forage for food, man," Brad says. "100% land living. That's the skill you need."

You nod, because you know that's true. But there are other

things that you need to survive, and by now you have those skills too.

730 nights.

730.25 lives.

You've been born into zombie worlds a dozen times, but you've survived the outbreak in six. You've run from diseased monsters, regular monsters, sad humans, angry humans. You've fought for kings, you've woven cloth for lords, you've farmed for your family. You've died from old age, the wrong mushroom, assassination, heartbreak, and snow. You know how to stitch a wound, cast a spell to stop a heart, ride a dragon, and perform the perfect curtsey.

But every time you die, every time you wake up in your dorm bed, you smile because this life is your favorite. You love Katherine's laugh and Brad is the best study buddy and shy Mary across the lounge from you is someone whose hand you'd like to hold one day. This life has electricity and the internet and is your first and longest. You never tire of it; you use your other lives to improve it.

The bottle comes your way. It's your turn to sip, to ask a question. "Who here is most likely to fail all their exams?"

This time, the group answer isn't you.

Spell Checker

You hate the language of magic. You don't mind speaking words for your spells, you don't mind the poetry of it, the richness of the sounds on your tongue. But the grammar of it is complicated and the fact that verbs and adjectives have prefixes *and* suffixes drive you mad.

You understand, of course. Magic must be precise. The world around you is order as well as chaos, and to prevent mishaps you have to describe things exactly. But humans didn't speak the language of magic naturally. It came from smaller tongues, wider mouths. Human practitioners are rare, undergo extensive speech therapy, and even then, still limit their spellwork because some conjugations are just so long you're bound to mispronounce something and ruin the spell.

You've lost more than one friend and colleague that way. Instead of putting a time bubble on a pot for a stew, Vanik had teleported himself to the bottom of the sea. Lesmi had flubbed the object on the verb, turning herself into a fish instead of the rock she'd found.

But this!

You eye what the fae is selling - xie won't let you touch. But you can see the inscription, read it, and find no fault in the words. A pendant you would wear pressed against your neck, whose magic would manipulate vocal cords, tongue placement, and breathing to force the right pronunciation out of your mouth. It's dangerous giving something else control over your body, but it's safer in an object than a spoken spell - no malicious will spoken into the words. You bargain down the price: if it doesn't work you could be dead, it's untested, you don't trust the demonstration. You eventually purchase it for the spell supplies in your basket and twelve monthly deliveries of foxglove and thyme picked during the week of a full moon.

Yes, this could save a life from a misspoken spell. But it could also, you think, open up more complex spellwork to you and that's worth the risk of the pendant.

You wait until you're home to try it and purposefully say a spell wrong. *Black* and *a dozen* sound similar, so you read a spell to summon a black bird but say one to summon a dozen birds. The pendant burns, your throat twitches, and you hear yourself say black.

You test it more, of course you do, and the spell checker only works if you read a spell. It has to know the correct one to force you to say. But it works! You write out complicated spells, feel your throat and face warm and move to say the words better. You've never felt this confident, never cast such big, complex spells. No longer do you limit yourself to one verb and one adjective. You create large and brown chairs. You scry to both listen and watch events in other locations. You order your meals to prepare themselves in single long sentences. You encourage plants to grow in particular places and particular directions.

Every spell you read is perfect.

But every word you say starts to feel wrong. You say "hello" and the choker shifts your mouth so the last vowel is accented. You mumble a recipe out loud to yourself, fingers trailing the English words, and your jaw clenches to change the resonance of sounds in your mouth. You say the name of a fae in the market so perfectly xie smiles at you, but your tongue jerks when you try to speak the baker's name.

You take the pendant off, and it helps, but there's residual power in your body from it. Your words still shift and spells are the only thing that feels right on your tongue. You put it back on.

Your English morphs to fae-accented words. You make your monthly delivery to the fae who sold you the spell checker, try to ask what the magic is doing. It was only supposed to help you pronounce spells right! Xie smiles at you, mouth wide. "It's spelled to help you speak correctly."

Xie speaks English better than you.

Occasionally, friends can't make out what you are trying to say. First words, then phrases.

You have gone beyond learning the language of magic. The words are still rich on your tongue, melted chocolate and vanilla, but the taste of them is no longer pleasant and powerful.

You wanted to speak fae perfectly. It is now the only language you can speak.

Highway Summons

The ritual requires a bell, a book, and a candle. Unfortunately, your car broke down in the middle of nowhere, and all you have is a cat toy, your car manual, and a spark plug. It'll still work, right? Probably?

You're not making it to the witch meet tonight. As you're new to the area, no one will know you haven't made it. And as you're new to witchery, you don't have the supplies you were hoping to borrow at the meet. Hopefully magic accepts substitutions.

You perform the spell, knowing your time to cast it is running out. It may not bring the perfect partner into your life, but you figure it'll still be someone who will love you and really, that's all you want after a string of heartbreaks.

Give me a lover who will brighten my life, you say as you dash a spark plug on the asphalt. *Give me a lover who can read my moods*, you cast as you rip apart the car manual as you have no candle to burn the paper. *Give me a lover whose laugh and mine can ring out together*, you whisper as you shake the hollow bird with a bell in the middle.

You sit there by the side of the road until the paper pieces scatter before calling a tow truck.

Results take at least twelve hours, according to your sources. You rest in anticipation.

When you go outside to eat lunch the next day, there's a cat curled up in the second chair of your patio set. You smile and coo at it, it meows back, and when its rough tongue tickles your fingers as you feed it a bit of fish, you know the magic sent you exactly what you needed.

Dragon Daydreams

Lord Charles's only daughter, Lady Marian, has been held by the dragon for forty-seven days. Four knights from the castle have left to rescue her and I wonder how many others throughout the kingdom have also left to fight. I strongly fear all who did are dead.

Sir David, who often wears Lady Marian's favor, was the first to leave. He used to keep one of her ribbons next to his chest during the joust. He most likely died with it still tucked into his armor. Those of virtue cannot commit suicide - it is the gravest of sins - but I'm sure she thought of it often. I wonder if Lady Marian hates herself for not being able to do it and calls herself a coward; so scared of death she cannot face it like the metal-clad men who visit.

I often ponder how the knights died. Crushed by an enormous foot perhaps, or speared by a claw, or roasted alive, baked in a suit of armor by a mouthful of flame. Or perchance slammed into a cliff by a tail, unable to rise, and life expired as they lay in a crumpled heap. I think, if the dragon had taken me, I would hide in a corner and avert my eyes. The sulfur-scented roar, the frightened screams of horses, and most dreadful of all, the much-too-still silence that descends after the sound of crunching bones and ripping meat ends would surely be too much for me.

But Lady Marian is more virtuous than I. She is, after all, the prisoner of a dragon. Perhaps she does what she can for the bold knights who arrive after days of traveling and using a saddle as a pillow. I can see her in my mind, hand gripping stone so hard its roughness causes her fingers to bleed, her dress in tatters. She would present herself to the most recent would-be champion to remind him of what he is there for and offer a silent support, a silent power, and then watch him die horrifically so that when she is free, she can tell his family about his valor. It is only after the knight has stopped moving that she will avert her eyes and move as far away as possible from the battle. Witnessing a fight to the death is one thing, but watching a dragon feed cannot be an appealing sight.

That is of course if she is still alive. It is quite possible that the knights who reach the dragon soon learn that they are not fighting to save honor but to avenge it. Or maybe they strive to prove it, the dragon's head the trophy instead of a woman with silk hands and full lips. I wonder if the bones they come across strike fear into their hearts or turn them into iron. How many knights walked the last part of the journey? I have heard of many a rider thrown because a horse smelled blood and refused to progress any farther.

I know I should not envy Lady Marian, her host and its hospitality cannot be pleasant, yet I still imagine myself in her place. Who would come to rescue me? How distraught would my mother be? Jealousy is a sin, I know, but oh! To be a name on hundreds of lips.

I wonder what shade of green are the dragon's scales.

Roommates

"Have you found it yet?" the demon hisses as I walk down into the basement.

"The terrifying thing you want me to kick out?" I say, scanning the shelving units for the outdoor Christmas decorations.

"Yessss."

In the darkest corner, the demon bubbles. I know he wants to eat me. He often says so, but he hasn't because he's convinced something in the attic would attack him back for doing so.

Last month though, his tune turned. No longer making threats about how he wanted to cook me, Mr. Basement Demon had asked for protection. The thing in the attic? It's growing stronger.

"I'm not gonna kick another supernatural creature out of my house," I tell the demon, "Especially if they're being a good roommate."

"Won't be good if it eatsss me."

"You wouldn't be good if you eat me either."

The demon says nothing and I huff, pulling down a trio of reindeer.

"Be back in a bit!" I shout as I heave it upstairs and outside.

Truth of the matter is, my house doesn't have an attic. It's a ranch, and the roof crawlspace is small enough I stay out of it. Not that I'd tell the demon. Not if whatever he's imagining has been keeping me undigested for the past eight months.

This is my first house. I refuse for it to be my only because something decided I belonged in its stomach.

Besides, by now I consider the demon my frienemy more than an actual pit of darkness that wants to swallow me whole. Sure, he likes to make threats. But he's always there to talk to.

I set the ladder next to the house and make sure it's secure. Then, I make four trips up it. The first three carefully carrying a reindeer and the last toting up my tools.

It doesn't take long for me to recognize that the clicks and snaps I hear aren't a result of me working.

"Hello?" I call out.

"Demon keeper?" something asks.

I swear and stand.

The demon is darkness in a basement corner. It bubbles and hisses, a concoction of evil as it likes to say. There's nothing like this here, the roof is too open.

A snap comes from the small metal heat vent. I peer between the metal slates.

It's hard to see at first. I'm looking for darkness, but eventually, I realize I'm not squinting at the sun on the other side, I'm squinting at something made of light. A crackling ball of light that's compacting, allowing me to see the inside of the vent.

Found my demon-checker.

"Yeah, that's me," I say, and the thing *clicks*.

It reminds me of my fireplace actually; the sounds it makes as the gas flames lick the fake wood. I thought the wood crackling noises were a stroke of fortune and good tech, not like there was anything actually burning, but now I am pretty sure I hadn't been hearing the fire at all. I'd been hearing this.

Great. A hungry, black hole in my basement and this ball of, fire probably, in my flue that I'd strengthened for a month ever since the seasons turned because I wanted the ambiance of flames.

"You're not gonna burn down my house, are you?"

The ball of fire-light snapped and I just knew it was thinking about it.

"It'd burn nice and warm." It flares, forcing me to shut my eyes for a second.

"You so much as move from this vent and I'll sic the demon on you, got it?"

"I know," it says.

Sensing Mr. Basement Demon is probably the only reason it hasn't. Just as the demon sensing this has kept me from being dinner.

I sigh. I don't want to make them play nice. I don't want to be caught between these things, whatever they are. But the demon and I are building a friendship. Maybe I could do the same with this thing too. Who knows, I might host a Thanksgiving for three next year.

Pillow Trades

It's not uncommon for you to fall asleep while scrolling the Internet, but usually your phone just falls to the mattress. Last night, you must have shoved it under your pillow because now it's gone and in its place is cash.

You regret the loss of your phone, of course, but the tooth fairy gave you brand new market price and so you buy a new used one with the cash and pocketed the rest.

You experiment. Sticking items under your pillow is better than the hassle of Facebook marketplace.

She doesn't take the plastic plate set you've tried to sell for weeks, but she takes a gold-rimmed china saucer from your Grandma's old set. You get brand new market value for it - from 1946 when it had been bought.

She ignores jeans and books, but trades for spoons and costume jewelry. The tooth fairy, you realize, is a bit of a magpie. If it's a little bit shiny, she'll give you cash.

You clear out the jewelry table at a garage sale, place them one by one under your pillow. The amount you get varies, but still is brand new market value of when the item was originally bought. Nothing more than $50, but that's better than the $8 you bought it for.

After a few weeks, something changes. Your bank account isn't as empty, your pillow is thicker. You take a nap, because sleeping on items isn't the most comfortable. You wake up to a crinkle, a note next to your nose.

The writing is tiny, you need your phone's magnifier to read it, but it turns out just as you've been using the tooth fairy, she wants to use you. She's dropped off a list of wants; hints at a finder fee in cash or precious metals.

It's specific, odd stuff. A clean dollar coin. A chandelier crystal. A reversible sequin pillow. Antique holiday ornaments. Photo hooks. All, you think, easy to get.

You sign her contract with a purple sparkly gel pen and offer it as a freebie.

Publication Notes

The majority of these stories have been published before, be it in other anthologies or shared online via my blog or social media channels.

Water Childe was in fact my first sale ever, to the podcast The Overcast, and I credit the market in kickstarting my career because it showed me there is an interest and market for fantasy short stories. A lot of credit for this particular anthology however has to go to - of all people – the Tumblr community who so enjoyed *Pillow Trades* it still gets reblogged a over a year later. Everyone who follows me there – thanks for both inspiring and motivating me!

If you enjoyed this collection yourself, please leave a review and call out your favorite story!

Thank you all!

Previous Market Publications:
Water Childe, The Overcast, (audio version) 2019

About the Author

Gwen Tolios is a Chicago-based author, staring at excel sheets by day and writing at night while trying to coax her cat to cuddle. While she got her start in short stories, Gwen has also written novels for children and adults.

For social media links and more, visit https://linktr.ee/gwentolios

Stay In The Loop

Sign up below to receive monthly updates on writing projects and book recs from Gwen Tolios. Never miss a new book (or sale!) from Gwen again.

https://gwentolios.substack.com/